DUNE™

HOUSE ATREIDES

4

Written by
Brian Herbert & **Kevin J. Anderson**

Illustrated by
Dev Pramanik

Lettered by
Ed Dukeshire

Colored by
Alex Guimarães

Cover by
Lorenzo De Felici

ABDOBOOKS.COM

Reinforced library bound edition published in 2022 by Spotlight, a division of ABDO, PO Box 398166, Minneapolis, Minnesota 55439. Spotlight produces high-quality reinforced library bound editions for schools and libraries. Published by agreement with BOOM! Studios.

Printed in the United States of America, North Mankato, Minnesota.
092021
012022

Library of Congress Control Number: 2021949530

Publisher's Cataloging-in-Publication Data

Names: Herbert, Brian; Anderson, Kevin J., authors. | Pramanik, Dev; Guimarães, Alex, illustrators.
Title: House Atreides/ writers: Brian Herbert and Kevin J. Anderson; art: Dev Pramanik and Alex Guimarães.
Description: Minneapolis, Minnesota: Spotlight, 2022 | Series: Dune
Summary: Set in the years leading up to the explosive events in Frank Herbert's Dune, this prequel series transports readers to the far future on the desert planet Arrakis where Pardot Kynes seeks its secrets; a violent coup is planned by the emperor's son; eight-year-old slave Duncan Idaho seeks to escape his cruel masters; and a young man named Leto Atreides begins a fateful journey.
Identifiers: ISBN 9781098251154 (#1, lib. bdg.) | ISBN 9781098251161 (#2, lib. bdg.) | ISBN 9781098251178 (#3, lib. bdg.) | ISBN 9781098251185 (#4, lib. bdg.)
Subjects: LCSH: Dune (Imaginary place)--Juvenile fiction. | Science fiction comic books, strips, etc--Juvenile fiction. | Life on other planets--Juvenile fiction. | Adventure stories--Juvenile fiction. | Graphic novels--Juvenile fiction.
Classification: DDC 741.5--dc23

Spotlight

A Division of ABDO
abdobooks.com

GIEDI PRIME
HARKONNEN HOMEWORLD

HUNTED AS SPORT FOR RABBAN.

I'LL SHOW HIM SPORT.

MY NAME IS *DUNCAN IDAHO.* AND I WILL SURVIVE.

THE HUNTER I KILLED WON'T NEED HIS MEDKIT ANYMORE.

JUST LIKE HE WON'T NEED HIS LASGUN RIFLE ANYMORE. IF ONLY--

KKKIZZAPPP

OOOPS...

HEAR THAT BLAST? HE'S THAT WAY, M'LORD RABBAN!

HE MURDERED ONE OF MY MEN, SO MAKE HIM *HURT* BEFORE YOU KILL HIM.

HE'S CUT OUT HIS TRACKER. FIND HIM ANYWAY.

I STAY *ALIVE*. MINUTE BY MINUTE. ONE STEP AHEAD OF THEM. I CAN SENSE THE HUNTERS COMING...

AND THERE'S SOMETHING ELSE OUT HERE... ANOTHER HUNTER...

GRRRRRR

BZZZZTTTTTT

THAT WAY! HE'S AN EIGHT-YEAR-OLD *CHILD* AND HE MAKES FOOLS OF YOU!

THEY THINK THIS IS A GAME.

MAYBE NOW THEY'LL PLAY *MY* GAME.

THAT FLASH... A *SIGNAL* OF SOME KIND? WHO COULD BE SIGNALING OUT HERE?

WHOEVER IT IS, THEY AREN'T RABBAN.

COULD BE MY ONLY CHANCE OUT OF HERE...

THEY'LL KEEP HUNTING, AND SOONER OR LATER...

I'LL SET ANOTHER TRAP...

I DON'T NEED MY HANDLIGHT OTHERWISE.

WHAT IS THIS?

HE'S OUT HERE SOME- WHERE.

GIEDI PRIME
HEADQUARTERS OF BARON HARKONNEN

I AM NO STRANGER TO DESPICABLE ACTS...

BUT I DESPISE THIS ONE.

WHY DOES SHE HAVE TO BE SO SMUG? I COULD KILL HER RIGHT NOW. SURELY PITER DE VRIES COULD FIND A WAY TO HIDE THE BODY...

I DO NOT ENJOY THIS EITHER, BARON. BUT I WILL HAVE A *CHILD* BY YOU.

THE SISTERHOOD DEMANDS IT.

OR I WILL DESTROY YOU WITH MY LITTLE FINGER.

I WILL GIVE YOU A VIAL OF MY DNA. THAT IS THE BEST I CAN DO.

NO, THE PREGNANCY MUST COME FROM NATURAL MEANS. THOSE ARE THE *RULES* OF THE BENE GESSERIT.

IF YOU NEED A HARKONNEN BLOODLINE, THEN ASK MY NEPHEW RABBAN. OR BETTER YET, HIS WEAKLING FATHER ABULURD BACK ON LANKIVEIL!

YOU KNOW THAT WILL NOT DO.

I FIND YOU *REPUGNANT!*

AS I FIND *YOU* REPUGNANT.

I HAVE THE ABILITY TO MANIPULATE MY BODY'S CHEMISTRY. I CAN BE CERTAIN TO CONCEIVE WITH ONLY ONE COUPLING.

MAKE IT QUICK, BARON...

PLANET IX
GRAND PALAIS OF HOUSE VERNIUS

NO REGULAR MOVEMENTS, PRINCE RHOMBUR. NOTHING THE MEK CAN PREDICT.

THUFIR HAWAT WOULD LOVE TO SEE A TRAINING SESSION LIKE THIS. MAYBE MY FATHER WILL PROCURE A FEW IXIAN TRAINING MEKS.

SCORE! DEACTIVATED! LEVEL SIX POINT FIVE!

YOUR PERSONAL BEST, MY PRINCE. THESE ADAPTIVE MEKS ARE VERY HARD TO DEFEAT.

GOOD SPARRING, RHOMBUR! YOU HAVE A GOOD TEACHER.

AND NOW IT'S YOUR TURN, LETO. SEE IF YOU CAN BEAT MY SCORE.

KAILEA! YOU NEVER COME TO WATCH TRAINING SESSIONS.

I NEVER COME TO WATCH *YOU*, BROTHER. BUT I WOULD LIKE TO SEE *LETO* FIGHT.

I AM UP TO THE TASK, LADY KAILEA.

THESE ADAPTIVE MEKS ARE A NEW DESIGN, AND I WANT MY FATHER TO BRING THEM TO MARKET. THEY CAN ANTICIPATE THE MOVES OF A HUMAN OPPONENT.

REMEMBER THE *STRICTURES* OF THE GREAT CONVENTION. "THOU SHALT NOT MAKE A MACHINE IN THE LIKENESS OF THE HUMAN MIND."

DON'T BE SILLY, LETO. ON IX, WE KNOW WHAT WE'RE DOING.

SIX DEAD HARKONNEN SOLDIERS...BUT I HAD TO HELP THOSE FREMEN MEN. THEY WOULD HAVE BEEN KILLED.

STILL, THIS COULD BE A PROBLEM...

ARRAKIS

THEY ARE TAKEN CARE OF.

TAKEN CARE OF...

THE CUT WAS DEEP. *STILGAR* IS GRAVELY WOUNDED, BUT HE WILL LIVE. I WILL TAKE HIM TO HELP.

WE KNOW WHO YOU ARE, IMPERIAL MAN. WHY DID YOU HELP US?

WHY? IT WAS THE RIGHT THING TO DO. I NEED--

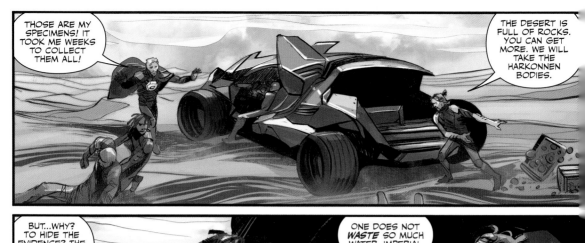

THOSE ARE MY SPECIMENS! IT TOOK ME WEEKS TO COLLECT THEM ALL!

THE DESERT IS FULL OF ROCKS. YOU CAN GET MORE. WE WILL TAKE THE HARKONNEN BODIES.

BUT...WHY? TO HIDE THE EVIDENCE? THE DESERT WILL DO THAT ALL BY ITSELF.

ONE DOES NOT *WASTE* SO MUCH WATER, IMPERIAL MAN.

WE WILL MAKE OUR OWN WAY. OMMUN WILL BE SWIFT, GETTING MEDICAL CARE FOR STILGAR.

WHAT IS YOUR NAME? SINCE WE ARE STRANDED HERE TOGETHER.

IS THERE A POINT TO EXCHANGING NAMES?

WELL, I DID JUST SAVE YOUR LIVES.

AH, THE *WATER BOND.*

FOLLOW ME, OR YOU WILL DIE. WE MUST MAKE IT TO THOSE ROCKS. WE WILL BE SAFE IN THE *SIETCH.*

WHAT'S A SIETCH?

YOU HAVE MUCH TO LEARN.

RED WALL SIETCH

I DO NOT LIKE THIS... AN ILL OMEN.

STILGAR WILL LIVE, *NAIB HEINAR*. THE STRANGER SAVED HIM.

THE STRANGER SAVED A CARELESS FOOL.

LOOK AT WHAT YOU HAVE BUILT HERE! WONDROUS SURVIVAL ADAPTATIONS FOR A HARSH ENVIRONMENT. DO THE FREMEN HAVE MANY OF THESE... SIETCHES?

YOU SHOULD NOT HAVE BROUGHT AN OFFWORLDER HERE.

HE FOUGHT HARKONNENS WITH US, NAIB. WHAT WERE WE SUPPOSED TO DO?

FASCINATING! YOU MANUFACTURE YOUR OWN *STILLSUITS?* OF COURSE YOU DO.

I WILL SEE WHAT THIS IMPERIAL MAN IS ABOUT. WE CAN ALWAYS TAKE HIS WATER LATER.

AH, I HAVE WANTED TO MEET THE FREMEN FOR SO LONG. I HAVE SO MUCH TO DISCUSS, SO MUCH TO LEARN.

I SMELL *SPICE*. YOU USE IT AS A BASE MATERIAL? AH, YOU MANUFACTURE PLASTICS. FABRICS, TOO?

THIS IS JUST WHAT I NEEDED TO KNOW. HOW MANY PEOPLE ARE THERE?

YOU CAN HELP ME WITH A *GRAND ENVIRONMENTAL PLAN*.

WHAT DO YOU *WANT* WITH US, IMPERIAL MAN?

I WANT TO TELL YOU MY DREAMS FOR ARRAKIS. FOR *DUNE!*

YOU CAN TALK--UNTIL THE COUNCIL DECIDES YOUR FATE!

I SEE NOTHING SPECIAL.

AHH, BECAUSE YOU ARE NOT SUPPOSED TO SEE ANYTHING SPECIAL.

ALL THOSE SHIPS BRING TAXES TO THE EMPEROR, DELEGATES TO ARGUE TRADE DEALS, BRIBES, EXPENSIVE CARGO. SOON ENOUGH...THE IMPERIUM WILL DELIVER THOSE TRIBUTES TO ME.

IF OLD ELROOD EVER DIES!

IT WILL TAKE TIME, MY FRIEND. THE N'KEE IS A SLOW POISON-- WE CHOSE IT THAT WAY INTENTIONALLY.

BUT OBSERVE CAREFULLY, AND YOU CAN ALREADY SEE THE EFFECTS ON THE OLD MAN, HIS TREMORS, HIS MOOD, HIS LACK OF FOCUS...

HE'S A MEAN, DODDERING OLD FOOL, WITH OR WITHOUT THE POISON. NOW EXPLAIN YOURSELF, HASIMIR. WHAT IS SO IMPORTANT ABOUT THAT *HEIGHLINER?*

IT CARRIES A VERY IMPORTANT COURIER, A REPRESENTATIVE WITH A VITAL MESSAGE THAT MAY WELL CHANGE THE SHAPE OF THE IMPERIUM.

WE HAVE ALREADY DISCUSSED, HMMMM, THE BENEFITS OF FINDING A SUBSTITUTE FOR THE SPICE MELANGE. A *SYNTHETIC ALTERNATIVE* TO BE CREATED IN A SOPHISTICATED LABORATORY ENVIRONMENT.

YOU MEAN THE FILTHY *TLEILAXU?* IT WAS A RIDICULOUS SUGGESTION. WHO WOULD WANT TO DO BUSINESS WITH SUCH VERMIN?

WHY, THE IMPERIUM, MY FRIEND. *YOU.* ONLY THE TLEILAXU HAVE THE BIOCHEMICAL SKILLS AND THE, AHH, ETHICAL FLEXIBILITY TO TAKE ON SUCH A TASK. BUT THEY WILL NEED TREMENDOUS RESOURCES TO SUCCEED.

I HAVE DISPATCHED A MESSENGER WITH A SIGNIFICANT BRIBE, REQUESTING THE BEST TLEILAXU RESEARCHER TO COME HERE. TO YOU. TO MAKE HIS PLAN.

I STILL DON'T LIKE IT, HASIMIR...

YOU WILL LIKE IT FINE WHEN WE BREAK THE *MONOPOLY* ON ARRAKIS AND DOMINATE THE SPACING GUILD, HMMMM?

DEEP UNDERGROUND IT'S IMPOSSIBLE TO TELL WHAT TIME OF DAY IT IS...BUT I ALWAYS WAKE EARLY. EVEN AFTER TWO MONTHS, MY BODY STILL REMEMBERS CALADAN...

RHOMBUR ISN'T MUCH COMPANY UNTIL LATE IN THE MORNING.

SLEEP ON, MY FRIEND. I HAVE TOO MUCH TO SEE!

I'VE LEARNED HOW TO EXPLORE THE UPPER BUILDINGS, HOW TO USE THE IXIAN TRANSPORT SYSTEMS...BUT *DOWN THERE*, WHERE THE COMMONERS LIVE AND WORK...

I'D RATHER SEE WITH MY OWN EYES.

SUBOID WORKERS... RHOMBUR SAYS THEY ARE A SKILLED LABOR FORCE, BUT THEY REMAIN HERE IN THE LOWER LEVELS.

HE SAYS HE'S NEVER MET ONE...

THE SUBOIDS FAR *OUTNUMBER* THE ADMINISTRATORS AND NOBLES, BUT RHOMBUR INSISTED THAT THEY'RE WELL TAKEN CARE OF.

THAT THEY'RE HAPPY...

MAYBE THEY'RE LIKE THE KINDLY PUNDI RICE FARMERS, OR THE CALADAN PRIMITIVES...

HELLO!

GIEDI PRIME
FOREST GUARD STATION

STOP STRUGGLING, BOY, OR I'LL THROW YOU BACK TO THE HARKONNENS!

WHO ARE YOU? WHY SHOULD I TRUST YOU?

WHAT HAVE YOU GOT TO LOSE? I'M GETTING YOU OUT OF HERE.

OH, RABBAN WILL HATE THIS! ALMOST AS MUCH AS I HATE HIM!

I EXPOSED SPIES AND TRAITORS AMONG THE GIEDI PRIME BUREAUCRATS, ANYBODY RABBAN WANTED TO GET RID OF.

HE PROMISED ME A GREAT REWARD. A PROMOTION.

THIS IS THE BEST WAY I CAN TWIST THE KNIFE IN HIS BACK--TAKE AWAY HIS LITTLE TOY! THAT'LL TEACH HIM TO CHEAT ME.

HOW I WISH I COULD SEE HIS FACE!

SO, YOU'RE NOT DOING THIS FOR ME AT ALL...

BUT AT LEAST I'M AWAY FROM HERE...

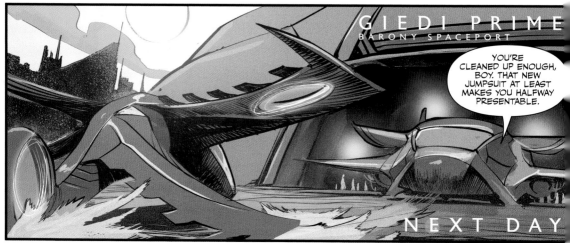

YOU'RE CLEANED UP ENOUGH, BOY. THAT NEW JUMPSUIT AT LEAST MAKES YOU HALFWAY PRESENTABLE.

NEXT DAY

I'M SURPRISED YOU DIDN'T JUST DUMP ME OUT IN THE CITY.

YOU CAN STILL BE USEFUL, HELP ME PAY ANOTHER DEBT.

RENNO! WHERE'S RENNO? TELL HIM I BROUGHT WHAT I PROMISED.

WHY SHOULDN'T I JUST RUN?

BECAUSE THEN YOU WOULD BE A FOOL. I'M GETTING YOU OFF-PLANET-- SHOW SOME APPRECIATION.

IS THIS THE SHIP-RAT YOU PROMISED ME, JANESS? I SUPPOSE HE CAN DO SOME OF THE FILTHY WORK THAT NEEDS DOING.

I'VE NEEDED HELP SINCE THE LAST ONE DIED.

WORK HIM AS HARD AS YOU WANT ON THE VOYAGE. JUST TAKE HIM TO WHERE IT'LL INFURIATE RABBAN THE MOST.

YOU PLAY DANGEROUS GAMES, JANESS...

COME, BOY, YOU CAN HELP US FINISH LOADING. WE'RE DEPARTING FOR CALADAN--

--THE HOME OF *HOUSE ATREIDES.*

TO BE CONTINUED...